TOMMY DONBAVAND

VIRUS

With illustrations by
Dan Chernett

First published in 2017 in Great Britain by
Barrington Stoke Ltd
18 Walker Street, Edinburgh, EH3 7LP

www.barringtonstoke.co.uk

This 4u2read edition based on *Virus* (Barrington Stoke, 2012)

ISBN: 978-1-78112-724-7

Printed in China by Leo

Contents

Chapter 1
A Site For Sore Eyes

M - y -

...

W - e - b - s - i - t - e -

...

b - y -

M -

...

"Where's the letter 'a'?" Max asked.

Nahim snatched the keyboard away before Max could type any more. Why had Mr Lee made him work with Max? Max was such a loser!

"Hey!" Max said. "Mr Lee said we had to work on this project in pairs!"

"If you want to waste the next hour on this, why don't you go and work with the girls?" Nahim asked. He turned to Amina and Polly at the next desk. They were typing and adding links to their own website.

"Do you two want to do a swap?" Nahim called out.

"What kind of swap?" Polly asked.

Nahim grinned. "You get Max," he said, "and I get to do something better than this 'build your first website' rubbish!"

"Nahim!" Mr Lee yelled. "See me after class!"

Nahim slumped in his chair. His face was like thunder.

Amina and Polly grinned.

"I can't work with the girls," Max said. "They go to stage school on Saturdays. I don't want to make a website about dancing. I want to work with you."

Nahim rolled his eyes. "So what do you want to make a website about?"

"*War Zone World*," Max said, with a big smile. "It's a game where you make your own avatar and go on adventures. My mum lets me play it after I've done my homework. I'm a 9th level wizard!"

"You're a 9th level loser!" Nahim muttered. He checked that Mr Lee wasn't watching, then began to type.

"What are you doing?" Max said. "Mr Lee said not to look at other websites. He said you could get a virus, and –"

"You only get viruses if you click on links you don't know," Nahim hissed. "But you've given me an idea ..."

Nahim grabbed his bag and began to root about in the bottom. "Please be there," he said. "Please be there ... Yes!"

Nahim pulled out a USB flash drive. He smiled, pushed it in and a few seconds later he attached a file called 'thunderstrike' to an email.

Max stared at the screen. "What's that?" he asked.

"A little treat for Polly and Amina. I'll teach them to laugh at me," Nahim said. Then he changed the file name to 'showtune'.

Max gasped. "That's a virus, isn't it?" he said. His eyes were wide. "You've sent the girls a virus that looks like a song!"

"Keep your voice down!" Nahim hissed. "I don't want Loony Lee to come over here!"

"But the school computers are all linked," Max said. "If the girls open that virus, every PC in this room will get it."

"Not just this room," Nahim said. "If I've got it right, the whole school network will grind to a halt – and they'll trace it to the girls' computer!"

And with that, Nahim clicked 'send'.

Amina was putting the details of the next stage-school show – *The Wizard of Oz* – onto her website when a window popped up on her screen.

"Showtune?" she read. "Is this yours, Polly?"

"Well, I did download some music," Polly said, and she reached for the mouse.

Amina pulled Polly's hand away before Polly could click on the link. "Wait!" she said. "Your music file is still there, look." She spun in her chair to face Nahim. "You sent us this," she said. "Didn't you?"

Nahim tried to look innocent. "Sent you what?"

"You're such a liar!" Amina said. "I bet this is a virus, and you wanted us to open it and infect every computer in this room!"

"Not just this room –" Max began.

"Shut up, geek!" Nahim snapped.

"Well," Amina said. "I'll just forward it to Mr Lee to look at."

Nahim dived for the girls' computer. "Don't do that!" he yelled. He grabbed the mouse and –

"He's trying to open the virus!" Amina told Polly and Max. She clamped her hand down on Nahim's. "If he does that, we'll all be in trouble!"

Max looked around. He was sure that Mr Lee would hear the racket and come running.

Click. Beep ... Beep ... Beep ...

Max turned towards the sound and ...

Nahim, Polly and Amina had vanished.

Chapter 2
Trapped in the Web

Nahim, Amina and Polly looked round in horror.

They were in a room where everything was yellow, even the floor. There were black patterns all over the back wall.

"What happened?" Amina gulped.

"I don't know," Polly said. "The classroom just vanished ..."

Amina looked at Nahim. "What did you do?" she demanded.

"Nothing!" Nahim yelled as he backed away. "This is nothing to do with me!"

"Rubbish!" Amina said. "Everything was fine till you opened that virus! Now everything's vanished!"

"But viruses can't do that!" Nahim said. "They can't change the real world."

"Well, the real world is nowhere to be seen," Amina said in a low and angry voice. "And it's your fault."

Polly took a few timid steps over the yellow floor. "Hello?" she called. "Is anybody there?"

No reply.

Polly slumped against the wall and tried not to cry. "Where are we?" she asked in a tiny voice.

Amina rushed over and put her arm around Polly. "I don't know," she admitted. "But I'm going to find out."

Then Nahim gasped. "Is your show *The Wizard of Oz*?" he asked.

Amina looked at him as if he'd gone crazy. "Yes," she said. "Why?"

"Those bricks behind you," Nahim said. "They've got letters on."

Amina ran her fingers over the bricks. They went all the way up to the roof. "He's right, Polly," she said. "Look – there's a letter on each one, sticking out from the bricks."

Nahim pointed at the wall. "If you read from the left of the wall, it says, 'Our next show is *The Wizard of Oz*. Try-outs will be on Saturday ...'"

Polly wiped her nose on her sleeve and joined the others. "I typed that onto our website before the rest of the world vanished," she said.

Amina bent down to read the next line. "'Be ready to dance at 10 a.m. Please wear loose clothes ...'"

"I typed that too," Polly said.

"Then I think I know where we are!" Nahim cried.

"Where?" Amina asked.

Nahim grinned. "We're inside your website!"

"No way!" said Polly. "How can that even happen?"

"I don't know," Nahim said. "But it has! Wicked!"

"Is this some sort of joke?" Amina snapped.

"What do you mean?" Nahim asked.

Amina glared at him. "You've somehow hidden the classroom to trick us into thinking we've been sucked inside the internet."

Nahim rolled his eyes. "So ... I got everyone to leave the room, painted everything yellow, built a wall of the exact letters you'd just typed – all in, like, zero seconds? Yeah, right."

Amina's face grew pale. Nahim was right – it sounded stupid. "OK," she said. "So – somehow – we're inside our own website. The question is – how do we get back out?"

"Who cares?" Nahim said. "It's cool! We're the first people to be inside the internet! Like the first men to walk on the moon!"

"One big difference," Amina said. "The first men on the moon knew how to get back home again."

This time, Polly did start to cry. "You mean we're stuck here for ever?" she sobbed.

Amina hugged Polly. "No," she told her. "We'll find a way back to school, I promise. Won't we, Nahim?"

"Are you two crazy?" Nahim asked. "No way – not yet! Think of all the different websites we can explore – videos, games, message boards ... We could go anywhere!"

"The only place we want to go is back to Mr Lee's class," Amina said. "And you're going to help us."

"Me?" Nahim said. "What makes you think I know how to –"

And that's when the ground began to shake.

Chapter 3
Climb or Die

It was hard for Polly, Amina and Nahim to stay on their feet.

"What's making this shake?" Polly screamed. She grabbed Amina's arm and held on.

"Er ... I think it's that." Nahim pointed to one side.

The girls stared in horror. "What *is* that?" Amina demanded.

A giant monster was stomping towards them. It had a twisted face like an angry bull's and sharp vampire teeth. It had scaly grey skin and horns grew from its head. The monster stopped and stared down at the three of them. Its eyes blazed red.

"I am your ruler!" it roared. Steam shot out of its nose. "You will serve me!"

Nahim found that he could speak despite his fear. "Who are you?"

The beast threw back its head. "I am the master of this domain!" it roared. "I am Thunderstrike!"

"Oh no," Nahim said in a tiny voice.

"What is it?" Amina asked.

Nahim stared up at Thunderstrike in terror. "It's my virus!"

Amina stared up at the monster as it scraped its claws across the yellow floor in a shower of golden sparks. "That's your virus?"

Nahim nodded. "That's what I called it – Thunderstrike!"

"You are an idiot!" Amina said.

"Bow down!" Thunderstrike bellowed.

"Why?" Nahim asked as he took a nervous step forward.

Amina tried to pull him back. "What are you doing?" she hissed.

"Getting us out of here!" Nahim stepped up to the monster. "I made you!" he yelled. "I made you from lines of code. "I am your master, and you will do what I say!"

Thunderstrike's eyes blazed with fury. He opened his mouth and roared. Nahim was covered from head to toe with gloopy strings of sticky green spit.

"Oh, yuck!" Nahim wiped the globs of spit from his face.

"Any other bright ideas?" Amina asked.

"Just one," Nahim said. "Climb!"

Nahim ran to the back wall and found a foot-hold on one of the letter bricks. He began to climb. The girls followed as Thunderstrike stomped after them.

"Hurry!" Amina cried. "We have to get higher!"

Thunderstrike reached the wall and swung a massive claw up at them. His claw hit Amina's shoe and tore a hole in it.

They climbed higher and higher, while Thunderstrike roared at them from below.

"Why doesn't he follow us?" Polly whispered.

"He's too big," Nahim said. "He can't grip onto the bricks."

Just then, the wall rocked. They clung on tight. Below them, Thunderstrike started to rip bricks out of the wall, to make holes for his giant claws. He was climbing after them!

"Sometimes I wish you'd keep your mouth shut, Nahim!" Amina yelled.

Thunderstrike was fast. He tore out brick after brick as he climbed.

They could feel his hot breath as he got closer.

At last, Nahim reached the top row of letters. He leaned down to pull Amina and Polly up.

"What now?" Polly asked.

Nahim looked up at a line of red letters above his head. "Are these your links?" he asked.

Amina nodded.

"Then we grab hold of one of them," Nahim said. "If we're lucky, it will send us to another website where we'll be safe."

"If we're lucky?" Amina cried. "You mean you don't know if it will work?"

"Only one way to find out!" Nahim stood and grabbed one of the bricks that made up the word 'Search'. As soon as he touched it, a tunnel of swirling colours opened up.

"Where does it lead?" Amina asked.

Nahim looked down at Thunderstrike. He was very close. "No idea!" he said. "But it can't be worse than here!" He took a deep breath, jumped into the spinning colours and vanished.

"I am your master!" Thunderstrike bellowed as he ripped bricks from below the girls. "You will serve me!"

"No way!" Amina shouted.

Then she and Polly jumped into the tunnel after Nahim.

Chapter 4
Creepy Crawlies

Amina, Polly and Nahim zoomed along the tunnel at top speed, flat on their backs. It was like the biggest water-slide in the world.

"Woo-hoo!" Nahim shouted.

"Are you enjoying this?" Amina said.

"Of course I am!" Nahim yelled. "We've escaped from Thunderstrike and now we're whizzing through cyber-space – this is much better than Mr Lee's boring old ICT class!"

The end of the tunnel rushed towards them and they tumbled out into another room. It was white with a long, thin box that hung in mid-air.

"What's this place?" Amina asked.

"A search engine?" Polly said. "That's what the link said – search."

"Cool!" Nahim said. He pulled a pen from his pocket and started to write in the box.

Amina pulled his hand away. "What are you doing?"

"I'm putting my name into the search engine," Nahim told her. "That way I can see how famous I am!"

"No way!" said Amina. "If this goes wrong – and everything has gone wrong so far – we could end up with a dozen Nahims running around. And we don't want that." She spotted Nahim's smile. "I said, we *don't* want that!"

"Oh, all right," Nahim moaned, and he rubbed out his name with his sleeve.

"Could we use the search engine to find a way home?" said Polly.

"Good idea," Amina said. "Perhaps this happened to someone else and they've posted info about how to find your way back." She took the marker pen from Nahim and wrote –

#
How do we get home?
#

"Now what?" Polly asked.

"Let's click on 'Search'," Nahim said. He looked around, then hurried over to a rectangle with 'GO!' on it. "Here we go ..." He pressed the button down hard.

A hole tore open in the wall next to Amina. It ripped like paper and a small metal spider crawled out.

"Oh!" Amina cried, as the spider scuttled away. "What's that?"

"A spider," Nahim said. "That's how search engines find things. Little programs called spiders crawl over the internet and collect information."

"But they're not *real* spiders, are they?" Polly said. Another hole ripped open in the floor and another metal spider clicked out.

"I don't think so ..." Nahim said, "but then I didn't think that computer viruses could come to life as angry monsters!"

Amina heard a ripping noise and spun round. There were five – no, six – more holes and six new silver spiders. As they watched, holes ripped open all around.

"I think we've got a problem!" Amina cried.

"You're not allergic to metal spiders, are you?" Nahim asked.

"Don't be stupid!" Amina snapped.

Dozens more spiders tore their way into the room. The floor was now a mass of shiny silver bodies.

"They're nothing to be scared of," Nahim said. "They collect data from websites, that's all."

"Really?" Amina said. "Then what's that one doing on your arm?"

Nahim yelped and brushed the spider off. It clattered to the floor, landed on its back and whirred madly as it tried to flip itself the right way up.

Polly screamed. Two spiders were climbing up her trousers.

"I told you we had a problem!" Amina said, as she knocked six spiders off her own body. "They think we're part of the website, and they're trying to find out what we are!"

More and more spiders began to crawl up their legs. Polly batted at them, but for every one she knocked off, three more took its place. In seconds, she, Nahim and Amina were covered from head to toe in the shimmering, clicking spiders.

"Have ... to ... get ... out!" Nahim panted, as spiders swarmed over his face. Their metal legs dug deep into his skin.

Then the world went black.

Chapter 5
Shop Till You Drop

Nahim came round on a hard stone floor. He groaned and sat up. "What's going on? Where are the spiders?"

"They've gone," said Amina.

"What? How?"

Amina smiled. "It was Polly," she said. "She stamped on one and smashed it open. They were full of links! We grabbed one and it opened up a tunnel and we dragged you in too."

"Thanks!" Nahim said to Polly. "So, where are we now?"

"I'm not sure," said Amina. "It looks like some kind of market place."

Nahim got to his feet. Amina was right. There were dozens of market stalls, all piled high with things. One had pairs of jeans. Another pots and pans. Others had toys, DVDs, pencils and more.

"If this is a market place," Nahim asked, "where are the shoppers?"

As if to answer his question, the arm of a huge crane swung down and sped over the market stalls until it reached one covered with kettles.

The crane jaws clamped around a kettle, then lifted it up into the sky and out of sight. Less than a second later, another crane arm swung down and zoomed along rows of hundreds of books.

"The cranes are the shoppers!" Amina said. She ducked as the arm swept over her head. Other cranes appeared from the clouds and snatched up items.

"Perhaps this is one of those auction sites!" Polly said. "My mum uses them to buy stuff for the house. She bids on things she wants and if her bid is the highest at the end, she wins –"

"Look out!" Nahim shouted, as a crane arm burst out of the clouds. But it was too late. In one swift move, the crane's metal jaws clamped around Polly and lifted her up into the sky.

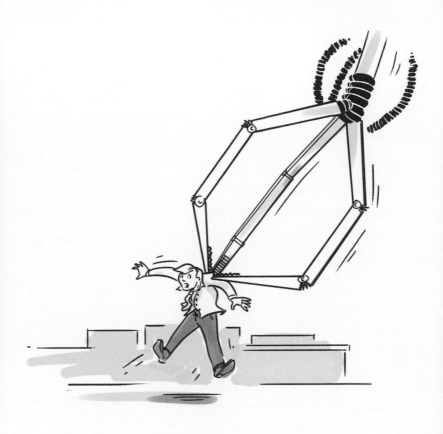

"Polly!" Amina cried as her friend was swept away. "Where's it taking her, Nahim?"

"She is coming to serve ME!" a voice boomed.

"Thunderstrike!" Nahim gulped. "Why is he here?"

"We have to follow Polly!" Amina yelled. "Look – another crane is heading this way. Jump on! Now!"

Nahim and Amina jumped into the air as the metal jaws of the crane whooshed past. The crane grabbed them and they clung on as it lifted them up and up. As they passed through thick clouds, they saw they were swinging towards a huge conveyor belt. When they were above it, the metal jaws opened and dropped them onto the belt along with dozens of items from the auction site.

"Where's Polly?" Amina said. She climbed onto a box of picture frames to get a better view.

"There!" Nahim said. "She's in the middle of a pile of teddy bears."

They dodged racks of fancy dress costumes and jumped over packs of nappies as they raced along the belt towards Polly. They reached her just as the items in front of her began to drop off the end of the belt into a huge bag marked 'Post'.

Polly was hugging one of the teddy bears and crying.

"Time to get out of here," Nahim said as he grabbed Polly's hand and pulled her to her feet. "You saved me, and now we've saved you!"

"Don't speak too soon!" Amina yelled, as the belt tipped the three of them off the end and into the big Post bag below.

Chapter 6
War Zone World

Amina landed on a box full of torches with a CRUNCH.

"Is everyone all right?" she called. She tried not to think about the poor person who had ordered the torches. They weren't going to be happy when the box arrived!

"I'm OK," Polly said. "I landed on a box of net curtains."

The sky disappeared as the Post bag was closed, but then Amina found a torch that still worked and switched it on.

"I wish I'd landed on curtains!" Nahim groaned. He crawled over the boxes to reach Polly and Amina. "Why is it always me that gets the messy stuff?" he moaned, and they saw that his hands and face were smeared in bright blue paint.

The girls laughed. "Well, at least we're on our way home now," said Amina. The boxes around them lurched as the bag began to move.

"No," Nahim said. "We have to get out! All this stuff is here to be posted. If we stay in the bag, we'll be posted, as well – to Thunderstrike!"

"But what can we do?" Polly asked. "It's not as if we can wave a magic wand and zap ourselves home."

"Maybe we can!" Nahim said.

"What do you mean?" said Polly, confused.

"Remember – Max is a 9th level wizard," Nahim said. "Perhaps he can cast a spell to get us back to school."

"You mean Max from our ICT class?" Polly asked. "He can do magic?"

"Not in real life," said Nahim. "He plays a wizard in an online game called *War Zone World*. If we can find him there, he might have the power to send us home!"

"Nice idea," said Amina. "But how do we find a link to *War Zone World* in here?"

"We don't!" Nahim grinned. "I'll make one!"

"Make one?" said Polly. "How?"

"Internet links are just groups of letters," Nahim said. "And look at all the parcels around us – they've all got addresses on. If we tear letters off the parcels, I can use them to write the code for a link to *War Zone World*. I'll need three letter 'w's to begin with ..."

For the next 15 minutes, the girls tore letters from the address labels on the parcels while Nahim laid them out on a long cardboard box.

"There!" he said at last. "That should do it!"

Amina looked at the home-made link.

#

<a href="http://www.warzoneworld.
com">Warzone World</a>

#

"Are you sure that'll work?" she asked.

"Trust me," Nahim said. "I'm an expert at website links." He took hold of the girls' hands. "Ready?"

"Let's do it!" Polly smiled. She grabbed hold of the link and the circle of spinning colours opened in front of them again.

"I take back what I said!" said Amina. "You're not an idiot – you're a genius!"

Nahim smiled. "At long last – my talents have been discovered!"

Then the three of them jumped into the tunnel of light together.

This time they stayed on their feet as they whizzed along, with their arms stretched out on either side to help keep their balance.

"I suppose this is why they call it 'surfing the internet'!" Polly yelled.

The end of the tunnel raced towards them and they jumped out. They landed in the middle of a forest.

"Is this it?" Amina asked. "Are we in *War Zone World*?"

"You are indeed!" a tiny voice answered. The children spun round to find a fairy hovering in the air behind them. "You look different to all the other players here," the fairy said. "What kind of characters are you?"

"We're elves," Nahim said, with a wink to Polly and Amina. "But we're on a secret quest and we have to stay in disguise."

The fairy buzzed around in a small circle. She seemed to believe him.

"Do you know how we can find a character called Max the Wizard?" Amina asked.

But before the fairy could reply, a dark shadow fell over the forest.

Chapter 7
Max

Thunderstrike crashed through the trees and glared down at the children.

"You should have known you could not escape!" he bellowed.

"I say!" the fairy said in its tiny voice. "I've never seen the likes of you around here bef–"

With a growl, Thunderstrike snatched the fairy out of the air, stuffed her into his mouth and crunched.

"Yuk! I think I'm going to be sick!" Amina groaned.

"Well, don't be sick on me!" Nahim said. "I've had too much gunk on me today already. Come on – run!"

They all turned and ran deeper into the forest. Thunderstrike chased after them, ripping up trees by the roots and tossing them away as if they were nothing but little twigs.

"I take back what I took back," Amina shouted at Nahim as she ran. "You're an idiot again!"

"I didn't know that thing would be waiting for us, did I?" Nahim cried. "I thought we could – OW!"

Amina and Polly stopped and turned. Nahim had tripped on a tree root and fallen over.

Thunderstrike was rushing towards him, eyes blazing.

The girls raced back to Nahim. "Get up!" Polly said. "Hurry!"

"I can't!" Nahim said. He gritted his teeth. "I've twisted my ankle!"

Thunderstrike crashed to a halt in front of them. "Now you are mine!" he roared and reached down with a huge claw.

"Not if I've got anything to do with it!" a voice cried.

A bolt of lightning shot from the trees and hit Thunderstrike hard in the chest. He staggered back.

Amina spun round. "Max!" she cried.

"That's Max?" Nahim said.

The man behind them was tall with long, white hair. He wore a deep purple robe and carried a wooden staff.

"Hi guys!" he said with a wink.

"Who dares to challenge me?" Thunderstrike screeched, charging at them again.

Max raised his staff and another bolt of lightning shot out, stronger than the first. It struck Thunderstrike in the stomach. Thunderstrike bent over and crashed to the ground.

"I am the Great Maximus!" Max said, with a proud smile.

"Yeah!" Nahim shouted. "He's our friend – and he's a 9th level wizard!"

"No, I'm 10th level now," said Max. "While you were gone, I invented a new spell that gave me enough attack points to go up a level."

"A new spell?" Polly said. "What does it do?"

The Great Maximus strode over to where Thunderstrike was rolling on the ground in agony. He pointed his staff down at the monster.

"It mixes magic with anti-virus software!" he said and fired again.

This time the lightning bolt was purple – the same colour as Max's robe. The charge hit Thunderstrike right between the eyes and the monster screamed ...

... then exploded.

The girls ducked as blood and guts flew up in the air and landed with a splash all over Nahim.

"Typical!" Nahim groaned. He picked something horrid off his face and threw it as far away as he could.

Amina and Polly ran over to Max. "Thank you!" they cried. "You saved us!"

The Great Maximus smiled. "It was nothing!" he said.

"Can you get us out of here?" Polly asked. "We want to go back to school!"

Nahim tested his sore ankle as he got to his feet. "For once, I agree with Polly and Amina," he said.

"You're already there!" Max beamed.

Amina looked around. All of a sudden, they weren't in the middle of a forest – they were in front of their computers in Mr Lee's classroom. It was like they'd never left, only Nahim was covered from head to toe in green saliva, blue paint and red monster guts. He slumped in his chair.

"That ... That was amazing!" said Polly.

Max slid the cursor over the 'shut down' button on his computer screen and clicked. "Easy when you know how!"

The bell rang for the end of the lesson. The four of them picked up their bags and headed for the door. That was when Mr Lee spotted the slimy mess all over one of his computer keyboards.

"Nahim!" he roared.

Our books are tested
for children and young people by
children and young people.

Thanks to everyone who consulted on
a manuscript for their time and effort in
helping us to make our books better
for our readers.